Publisher's Foreword

The American artist Peter Newell (1862-1924) began his career drawing portraits, using crayons as his medium. Later, in addition to his own humorous pieces, he illustrated Mark Twain's *Innocents Abroad* and Lewis Carroll's *Alice in Wonderland* and *Through the Looking Glass*. His work is noted for its imagination and originality; authorities have found it difficult to pinpoint any definite influences on his artistic career.

The Hole Book, first published in 1908 by Harper & Row, was one of several works of verse and accompanying pictures by Newell. Our earlier reprint editions of his *Slant Book* and *Rocket Book* have proved so popular that we could not help but feel it appropriate to offer modern readers a further opportunity to appreciate the artist's unique humor.

THE HOLE BOOK

by PETER NEWELL

TUTTLE PUBLISHING
Tokyo • Rutland, Vermont • Singapore

Tom Potts was fooling with a gun
   (Such follies should not be),
When—bang! the pesky thing went off
   Most unexpectedly!

Tom didn't know 'twas loaded, and
   It scared him 'most to death—
He tumbled flat upon the floor
   And fairly gasped for breath.

The bullet smashed a fine French clock
   (The clock had just struck three),
Then made a hole clean through the wall,
   As you can plainly see.

Out in the kitchen Bridget Quinn
   Was busying about,
When through the boiler crashed the shot
   And let the water out!

●

The floor was flooded like a pond,
   The room was filled with steam,
And Bridget gathered up her skirts
   And rushed out with a scream.

Out in the back yard Sister Sue,
  With " Sis " and Mabel Dunn,
Was swinging underneath the trees,
  And having lots of fun,—

●

When—zip ! the speeding bullet sang,
  And cut the rope in two,
Then hurtled through the high board fence,
  And to the ground came Sue !

Just then an automobile passed,
  Its body painted green—
The bullet struck its side and pierced
  The tank of gasolene.

●

A loud explosion followed and
  A tremor shook the air!
The passengers were tossed aloft
  Amidst the smoke and glare!

An artist in a studio,
  Who had a medal won,
Was painting on " A Laughing Boy,"
  Which work was all but done :

●

The ball of lead this picture smote,
  As through the room it ranged,
And through the canvas bored its way,
  And the expression changed!

Old Granny Fink was sound asleep—
  As sound as one could wish ;
Beside her an aquarium
  Was standing, stocked with fish:

●

The bullet struck the crystal globe,
  And roused her from her nap—
And Granny found that she was drenched,
  With goldfish in her lap!

A lady came into a store
   Where animals were sold,
To buy a parrot with a tongue
   That wouldn't swear or scold;

●

But as she talked about the bird
   And asked about the price,
The bullet plunged clean through a box
   And freed a lot of mice!

Old Hagenschmit, behind his house,
  His new Dutch pipe was trying,
When—bing! the bullet smashed the bowl
  And sent the pieces flying!

●

"Who put dot bombshell in my pipe?"
  Exclaimed the startled smoker.
"If I could git my hands on him,
  Dere would be vone less joker!"

A pear-tree, seen above the wall,
 With fruit was laden down,
And Ned, below, appeared to be
 The saddest boy in town;

●

Just then the restless bullet passed,
 And clipped a branching limb
Which bore a dozen pears or more
 And passed it down to him!

G. Foozleman, in high silk hat,
    Along the street was trailing,
When through the crown the bullet sped
    And sent his hat a-sailing!

●

" What do you mean, sir," blurted he,
    To Harvey Jones, behind him,
" By knocking off my high silk hat?"
    But Harvey didn't mind him.

Dick Bumble, with a bag of grain,
  Was going out to grind it,
When through the bag the bullet tore
  And left a hole behind it!

●

Dick neither knew the bag was pinked,
  Nor that a hole was in it,
And wondered why the load he bore
  Grew lighter every minute.

Tim Nickleby had hooked a fish,
　And was about to land it,
When—snap! his fish-pole broke in two—
　He couldn't understand it.

●

Of course the bullet did the trick:—
　It would have been more thrilling
If it had punctured Timothy,
　Who was in need of drilling.

A restless wild-cat had escaped,
   And roamed the gardens free;
The keeper, frightened at the sight,
   Had climbed a lofty tree:

●

The savage brute espied him there,
   And with an agile bound,
It met the bullet in the air,
   And tumbled to the ground!

A vender of balloons, a chap
  In Russia born and bred,
Came ambling through the dusty street,
  His wares above his head.

●

"Balloons! Balloons! Who vants to buy?"
  He shrilly cried. "I say—"
Just then his enterprise collapsed—
  The shot had come that way.

A German band was on parade,
   And all the district knew it,
When—boom! the bass-drum sounded out—
   The shot had gone clean through it!

●

The leader turned about in ire,
   And pointing at the drummer,
Exclaimed: "You sthart too soon, my friendt—
   You make a better plumber!"

Mis' Silverman had built a fire
  And shovelled on some coal,
When through the stove-pipe crashed the shot
  And made a gaping hole!

●

The smoke in murky columns rose,
  The lady raised a shout;
Then on the scene the firemen came,
  And put the lady out!

A cat espied a tiny mouse,
  And crouched to make a spring:
The mousey couldn't find a place
  In which to hide—poor thing!

●

Just then the bullet made a hole—
  A fair-sized hole at that—
And in it dashed the frightened mouse,
  And thus escaped the cat.

A thief was stealing in the door—
  A clever chap was he;
For he had waited till the gong
  Had summoned all to tea.

●

But at that moment came the shot,
  And smote the door-bell clear—
The butler reached the door in time
  To see him disappear!

Old Sandy, on his Highland pipes,
  Was drooning " Robin Hood,"
And coaxing from the boys and girls
  Such pennies as he could,—

When suddenly the bag went "squash!"
  The drone became a sigh—
The fleeting shot had pierced the bag
  Of wind in passing by!

For some excitement, good and hot,
  These lads were fairly spoiling,
When through the bee-hive plunked the shot,
  And set the pot a-boiling!

●

The startled swarm came streaming out
  In temper hot and baneful,
And drove the foe in awful rout,
  With volleys sharp and painful!

When Felix Fenno flew his kite,
   He found his hands were full;
It seemed determined to escape,
   So strongly did it pull.

●

But presently the whizzing shot
   The kite-string neatly parted,
And, like an air-ship on a cruise,
   His precious kite departed!

The grocer boy was teasing Snip
  By pelting him with rice,
And keeping just beyond his reach—
  Which wasn't very nice.

●

Just then the bullet clipped the chain
  That held the pup, and—joy!
He fairly sprinted through the air,
  And nabbed that grocer boy!

Mis' Newlywed had made a cake,
  With icings good and stout—
The bullet struck its armor belt,
  And meekly flattened out.

And this was lucky for Tom Potts,
  The boy who fired the shot—
It might have gone clean round the world
  And killed him on the spot.

Published by Tuttle Publishing, an imprint of Periplus Editions (HK)Ltd. with editorial offices at 364 Innovation Drive, North Clarendon, VT 05759 USA and 61 Tai Seng Avenue #02-12 Singapore 534167.

LCCCard No. 84-052396
ISBN 978-0-8048-1498-0

Printed in Malaysia

Distributed by:

Japan
Tuttle Publishing
Yaekari Building, 3rd Floor
5-4-12 Osaki, Shinagawa-ku
Tokyo 141-0032
Tel: (81) 35437 0171 Fax:(81) 35437 0755
Email: tuttle-sales@gol.com

North America, Latin America & Europe
Tuttle Publishing
364 Innovation Drive
North Clarendon, VT 05759-9436 USA
Tel: 1 (802)773 8930 Fax: 1 (802) 773 6993
Email: info@tuttlepublishing.com
www.tuttlepublishing.com

Asia Pacific
Berkeley Books Pte. Ltd.
61 Tai Seng Avenue #02-12
Singapore 534167
Tel: (65)6280 1330 Fax:(65)6280 6290
Email: inquiries@periplus.com.sg
www.periplus.com.sg

12 11 10 09 08
8 7 6 5 4 3 2

TUTTLE PUBLISHING® is a registered trademark of Tuttle Publishing,
a division of Periplus Editions (HK) Ltd.